WRITERS REPUBLIC

TALES OF LITTLE DAVE

ROBERT T. SAMUEL

This publication contains the opinions and ideas of its author. It is intended to provide helpful and informative material on the subjects addressed in the publication. The author and publisher specifically disclaim all responsibility for any liability, loss, or risk, personal or otherwise, which is incurred as a consequence, directly or indirectly, of the use and application of any of the contents of this book.

WRITERS REPUBLIC L.L.C.
515 Summit Ave. Unit R1
Union City, NJ 07087, USA

Website: *www.writersrepublic.com*
Hotline: *1-877-656-6838*
Email: *info@writersrepublic.com*

Ordering Information:
Quantity sales. Special discounts are available on quantity purchases by corporations, associations, and others. For details, contact the publisher at the address above.

Library of Congress Control Number: 2021932801
ISBN-13: 978-1-63728-203-8 [Paperback Edition]
978-1-63728-204-5 [Digital Edition]

Rev. date: 02/08/2021

Dedicated to my
nieces and nephews

Love,
Your Uncle

Once in a far-off forest,
there lived a rabbit named Becket.
On the outside he was a normal-looking
rabbit, but looks can be deceiving. For
Becket Rabbit was a magic rabbit.

One day Becket Rabbit was hopping through the forest when a big orange cat pounced on him and said he was going to "Eat him up."

Becket Rabbit said, "Mr. Cat, you don't want to eat me. I'm the only one who can take you home, and I can tell you are lost."

The cat said, "I doubt you could take me home. I think I'll just eat you."

Becket Rabbit replied, "Very well then eat me, but your house wouldn't happen to have a white picket fence and a pink window, would it?"

The cat was astonished, for indeed, his house had those very things. He let Becket Rabbit go and said, "All right, rabbit, take me home and I won't eat you."

Becket Rabbit stuck his furry paw out to shake the cat's even furrier paw and said,

"My name's Becket. What's yours?"

The cat said, "My name's Dave, but some people call me Little Dave."

And away they went.

They went through fields of
blue and purple flowers,

through green grass with little
pink flowers popping up,

across fallen trees covered with moss and tiny
mushrooms, and through thick bushes and trees.
But never once did Becket Rabbit try to
run. He stayed true to his word.

Finally, they came along a big river with little fish jumping in it and blue birds chirp-chirping on a nearby tree.

Thankfully, there was a log across it, so Becket Rabbit hopped across to the other side of the river. Little Dave was terrified of water, so as bravely as he could, he started to cross the river.

But the log rolled, and in toppled
Little Dave, right into the river.

Little Dave tried to get to the shore,

but the current was too strong.

Becket Rabbit ran along the shore shouting

encouragement to Little Dave.

Suddenly, the blue birds that had been chirp-chirping on the tree above him flew down and picked him right up out of the water.

Little Dave was choking on all the water in his lungs, so Becket Rabbit thump-thumped his belly until Little Dave spit the water out.

Little Dave got up and thanked the
blue birds and Becket Rabbit,
and he said, "How can I ever repay you?
I would have eaten you, given the chance,
but you saved me. I promise to never hurt
another living thing as long as I live."
And away Becket Rabbit and Little Dave
went, looking like true friends.

It was getting dark when Little Dave recognized a white picket fence and a pink window.
He turned to Becket Rabbit and gave him a hug and said, "If you ever need anything, just come on by. You are always welcome. And let me know if any other cats give you any trouble."
And so Becket Rabbit and Little Dave went their separate ways—

Becket Rabbit into the deep green forest

and Little Dave into his house, to curl up next to the fire after his long journey.

CPSIA information can be obtained
at www.ICGtesting.com
Printed in the USA
BVHW020728120421
604722BV00012B/129

9 781637 282038